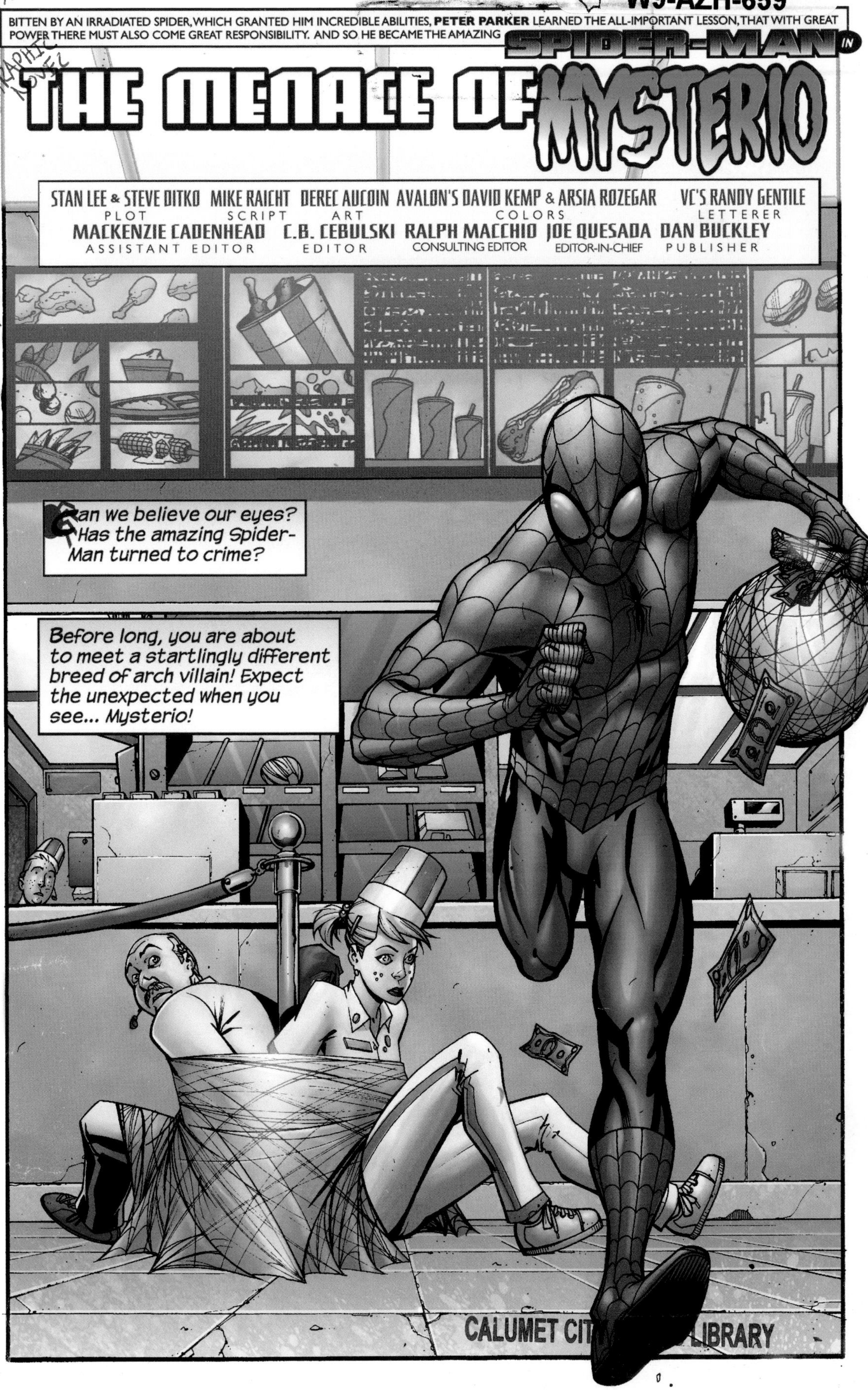
BITTEN BY AN IRRADIATED SPIDER, WHICH GRANTED HIM INCREDIBLE ABILITIES, PETER PARKER LEARNED THE ALL-IMPORTANT LESSON, THAT WITH GREAT POWER THERE MUST ALSO COME GREAT RESPONSIBILITY. AND SO HE BECAME THE AMAZING
SPIDER-MAN IN
THE MENACE OF MYSTERIO
STAN LEE & STEVE DITKO PLOT
MIKE RAICHT SCRIPT
DEREC AUCOIN ART
AVALON'S DAVID KEMP & ARSIA ROZEGAR COLORS
VC'S RANDY GENTILE LETTERER
MACKENZIE CADENHEAD ASSISTANT EDITOR
C.B. CEBULSKI EDITOR
RALPH MACCHIO CONSULTING EDITOR
JOE QUESADA EDITOR-IN-CHIEF
DAN BUCKLEY PUBLISHER
Can we believe our eyes? Has the amazing Spider-Man turned to crime?
Before long, you are about to meet a startlingly different breed of arch villain! Expect the unexpected when you see... Mysterio!

VISIT US AT
www.abdopub.com

Spotlight, a division of ABDO Publishing Company Inc., is the school and library distributor of the Marvel Entertainment books.

Library bound edition © 2006

Library of Congress Cataloging-in-Publication Data

The Menace of Mysterio!

ISBN 1-59961-022-1   (Reinforced Library Bound Edition)

All Spotlight books are reinforced library binding and manufactured in the United States of America

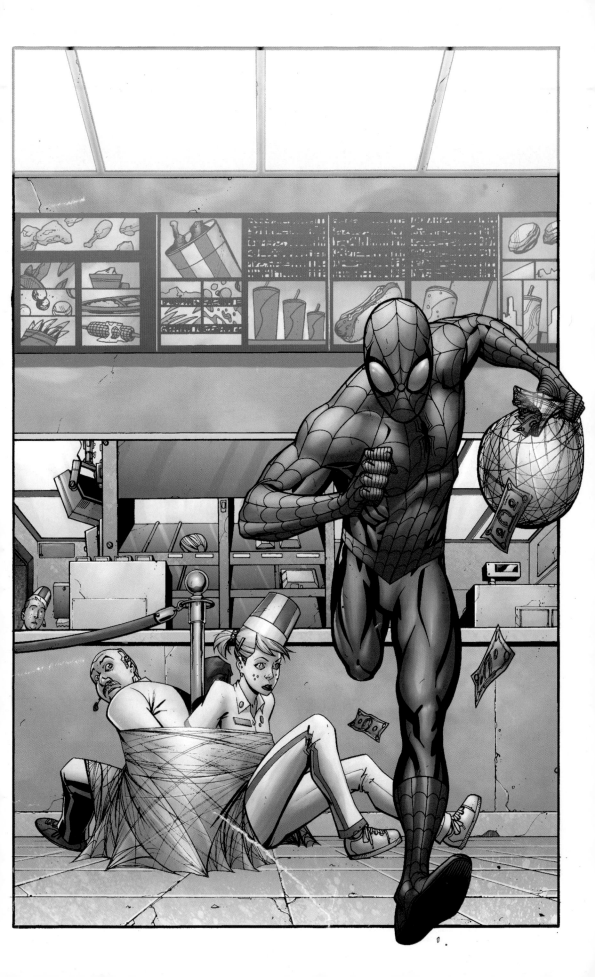

There's no way the Knicks should have traded--

HELP!

Spider-Man ripped us off!

What th--?

Call it in quick!

It's Spider-Man!

Hey! Stop!

This is McGregor and Lewis on 40th and Park--

Whoa!

--reporting a suspected robbery in progress!

We have an officer down and Spider-Man is swinging down Park Ave and--

I'm not down. I'm fine.

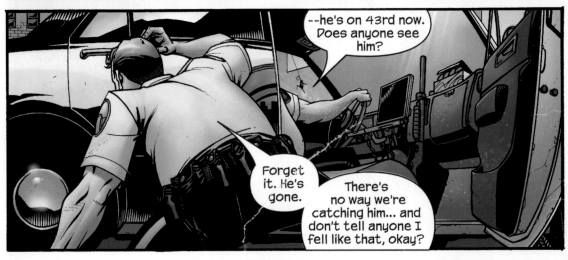

--he's on 43rd now. Does anyone see him?

Forget it. He's gone.

There's no way we're catching him... and don't tell anyone I fell like that, okay?

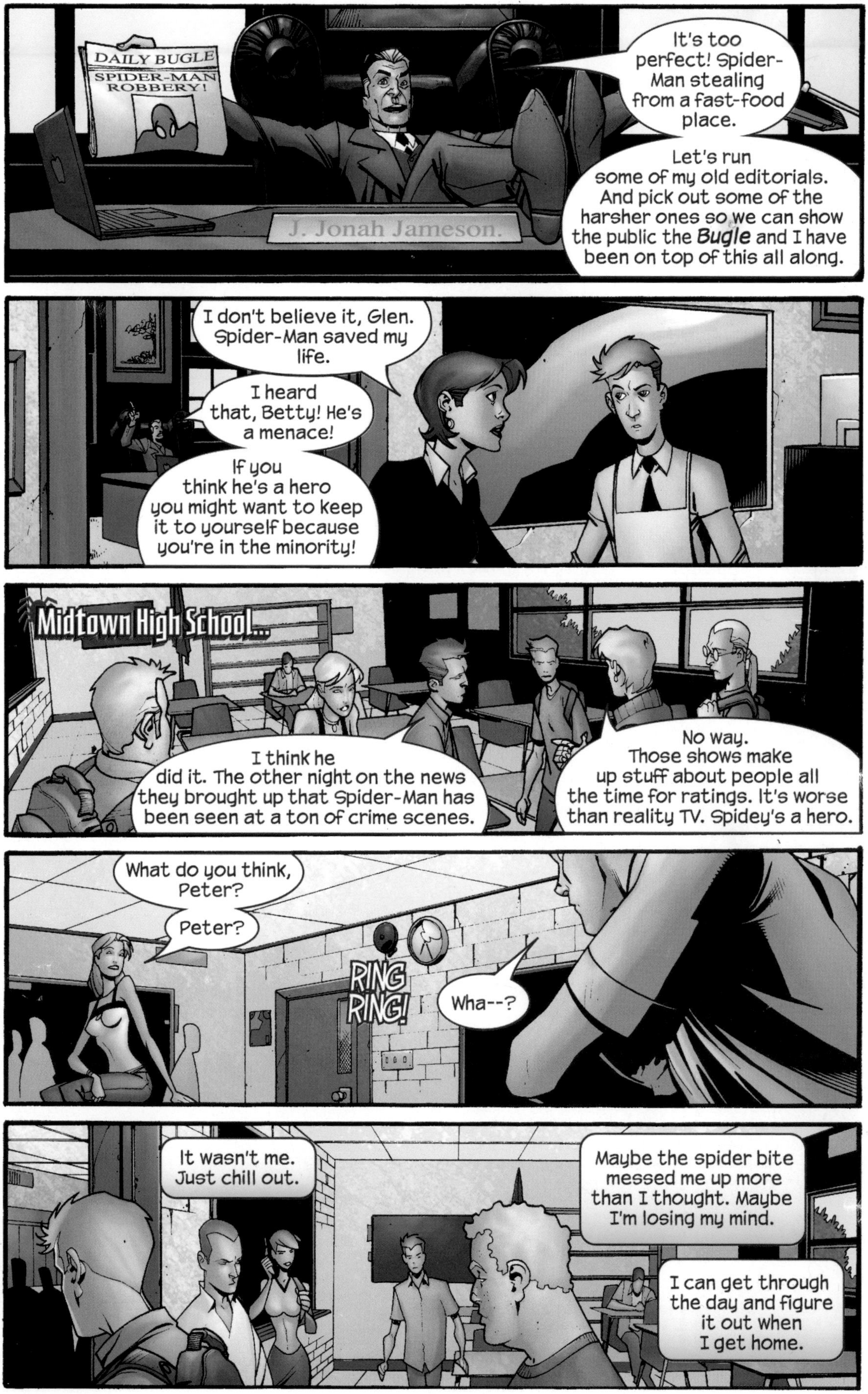
DAILY BUGLE
SPIDER-MAN ROBBERY!
J. Jonah Jameson.
It's too perfect! Spider-Man stealing from a fast-food place.
Let's run some of my old editorials. And pick out some of the harsher ones so we can show the public the *Bugle* and I have been on top of this all along.
I don't believe it, Glen. Spider-Man saved my life.
I heard that, Betty! He's a menace!
If you think he's a hero you might want to keep it to yourself because you're in the minority!
Midtown High School...
I think he did it. The other night on the news they brought up that Spider-Man has been seen at a ton of crime scenes.
No way. Those shows make up stuff about people all the time for ratings. It's worse than reality TV. Spidey's a hero.
What do you think, Peter?
Peter?
RING RING!
Wha--?
It wasn't me. Just chill out.
Maybe the spider bite messed me up more than I thought. Maybe I'm losing my mind.
I can get through the day and figure it out when I get home.

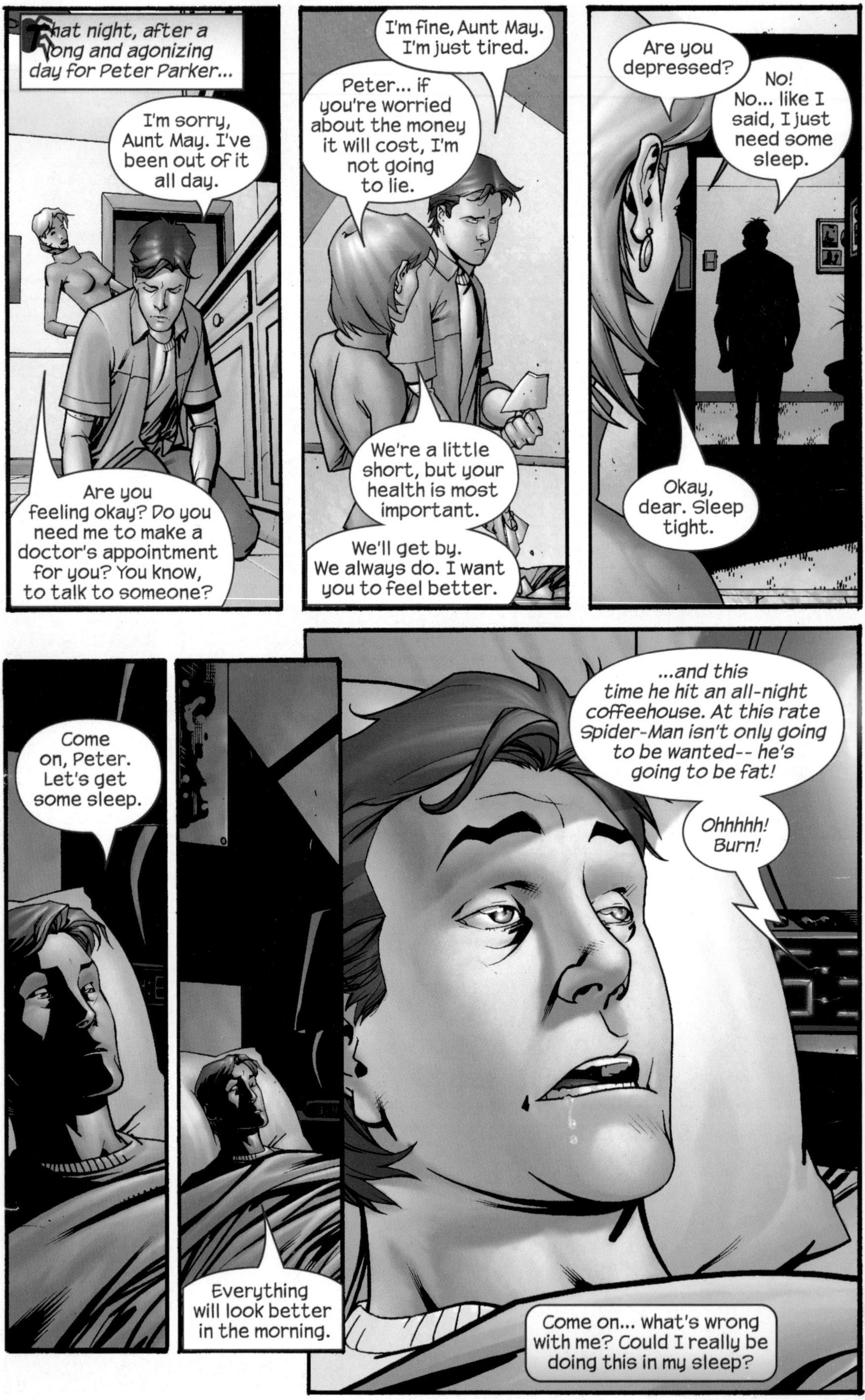
That night, after a long and agonizing day for Peter Parker...
I'm sorry, Aunt May. I've been out of it all day.
Are you feeling okay? Do you need me to make a doctor's appointment for you? You know, to talk to someone?
I'm fine, Aunt May. I'm just tired.
Peter... if you're worried about the money it will cost, I'm not going to lie.
We're a little short, but your health is most important.
We'll get by. We always do. I want you to feel better.
Are you depressed?
No! No... like I said, I just need some sleep.
Okay, dear. Sleep tight.
Come on, Peter. Let's get some sleep.
Everything will look better in the morning.
...and this time he hit an all-night coffeehouse. At this rate Spider-Man isn't only going to be wanted-- he's going to be fat!
Ohhhhh! Burn!
Come on... what's wrong with me? Could I really be doing this in my sleep?

Later that morning. The Daily Bugle.

Hey, Peter. Are you okay? You look pretty beat.

I'm fine.

Were you out late on a big date?

Did that Liz girl finally come around?

No... I was... I just can't talk right now?

Are you sure you don't need to talk?

Seriously, Betty. I appreciate your concern but you don't understand...

I can't help if you won't talk to me about it.

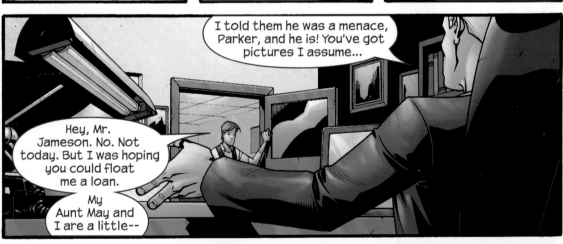

I told them he was a menace, Parker, and he is! You've got pictures I assume...

Hey, Mr. Jameson. No. Not today. But I was hoping you could float me a loan.

My Aunt May and I are a little--

The best way to get money is to earn it, son.

You're a go-getter, Parker. Go get me some pictures of Spider-Man stealing something.

And then you'll get paid.

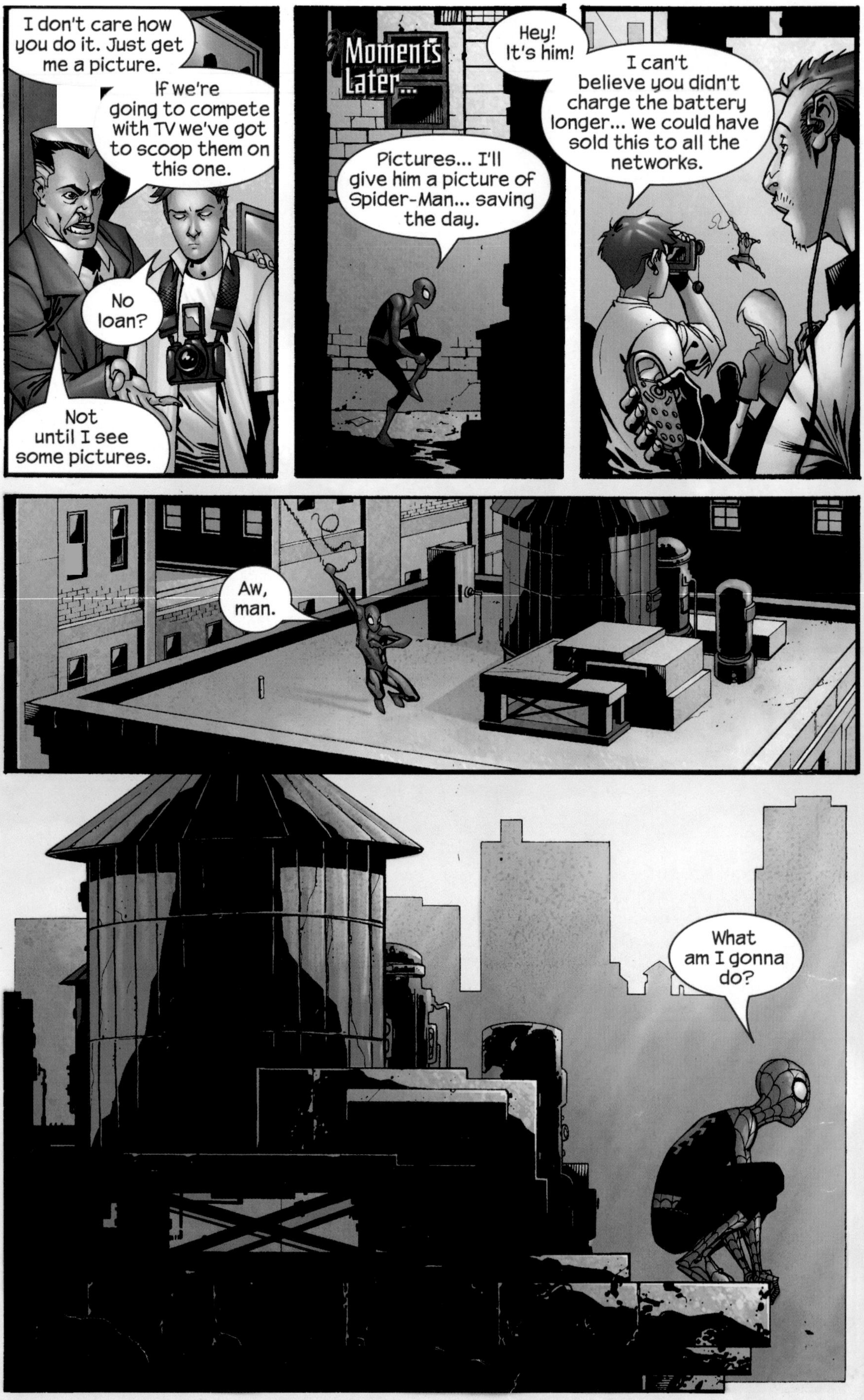
I don't care how you do it. Just get me a picture.
If we're going to compete with TV we've got to scoop them on this one.
No loan?
Not until I see some pictures.
Moments Later...
Pictures... I'll give him a picture of Spider-Man... saving the day.
Hey! It's him!
I can't believe you didn't charge the battery longer... we could have sold this to all the networks.
Aw, man.
What am I gonna do?

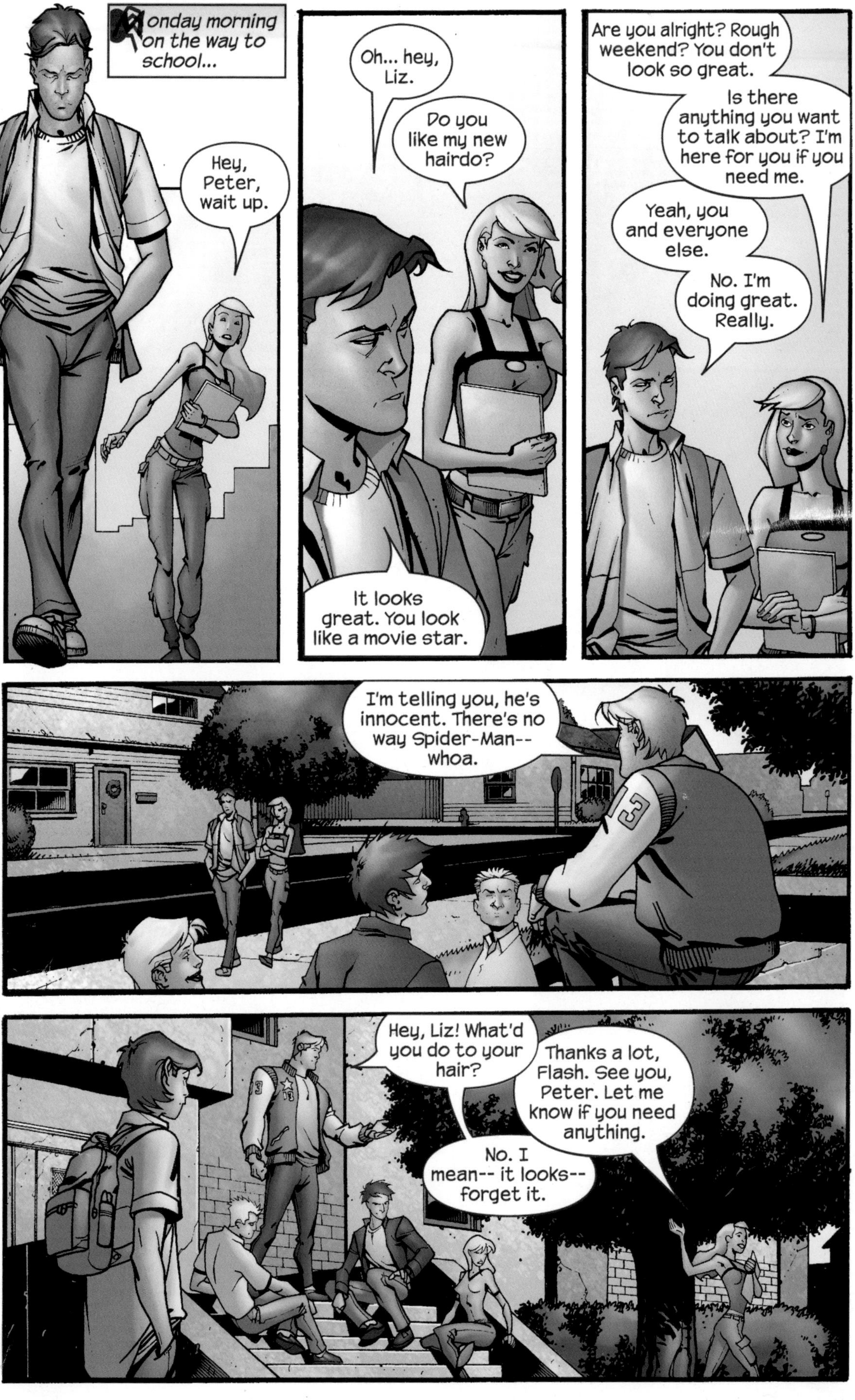
Monday morning on the way to school...
Hey, Peter, wait up.
Oh... hey, Liz.
Do you like my new hairdo?
It looks great. You look like a movie star.
Are you alright? Rough weekend? You don't look so great.
Is there anything you want to talk about? I'm here for you if you need me.
Yeah, you and everyone else.
No. I'm doing great. Really.
I'm telling you, he's innocent. There's no way Spider-Man-- whoa.
Hey, Liz! What'd you do to your hair?
Thanks a lot, Flash. See you, Peter. Let me know if you need anything.
No. I mean-- it looks-- forget it.

In JJJ's office...

I don't know. Some nutso sent me an e-mail and said he had some news about Spider-Man and he wanted to give the *Bugle* the scoop.

What's going --?

I am Mysterio!

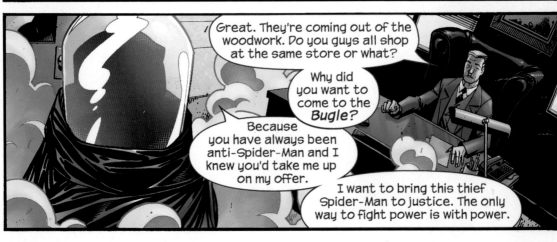

Great. They're coming out of the woodwork. Do you guys all shop at the same store or what?

Why did you want to come to the *Bugle*?

Because you have always been anti-Spider-Man and I knew you'd take me up on my offer.

I want to bring this thief Spider-Man to justice. The only way to fight power is with power.

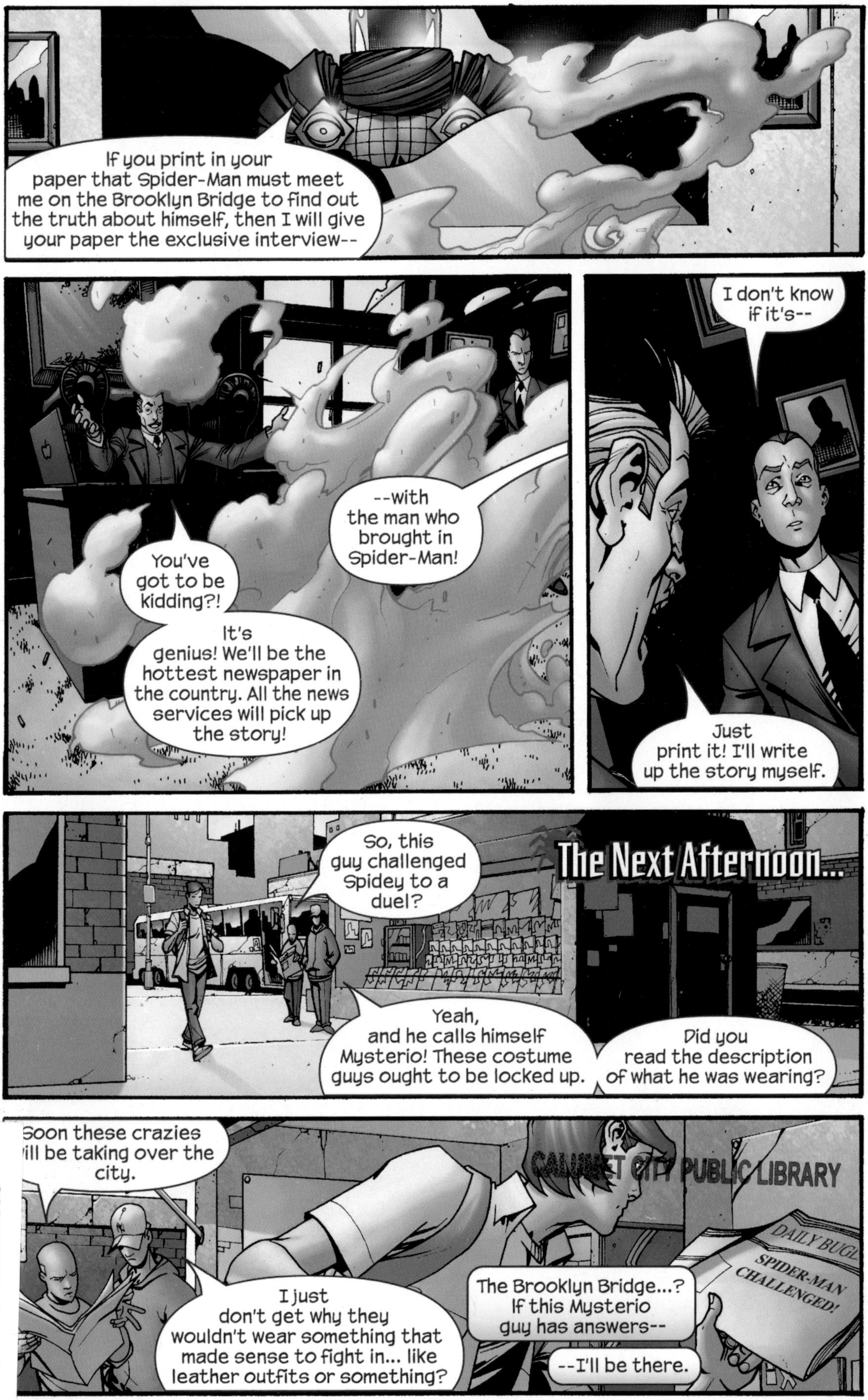

If you print in your paper that Spider-Man must meet me on the Brooklyn Bridge to find out the truth about himself, then I will give your paper the exclusive interview--
You've got to be kidding?!
--with the man who brought in Spider-Man!
It's genius! We'll be the hottest newspaper in the country. All the news services will pick up the story!
I don't know if it's--
Just print it! I'll write up the story myself.
The Next Afternoon...
So, this guy challenged Spidey to a duel?
Yeah, and he calls himself Mysterio! These costume guys ought to be locked up.
Did you read the description of what he was wearing?
Soon these crazies ill be taking over the city.
PUBLIC LIBRARY
I just don't get why they wouldn't wear something that made sense to fight in... like leather outfits or something?
The Brooklyn Bridge...? If this Mysterio guy has answers--
--I'll be there.
SPIDER-MAN CHALLENGED!

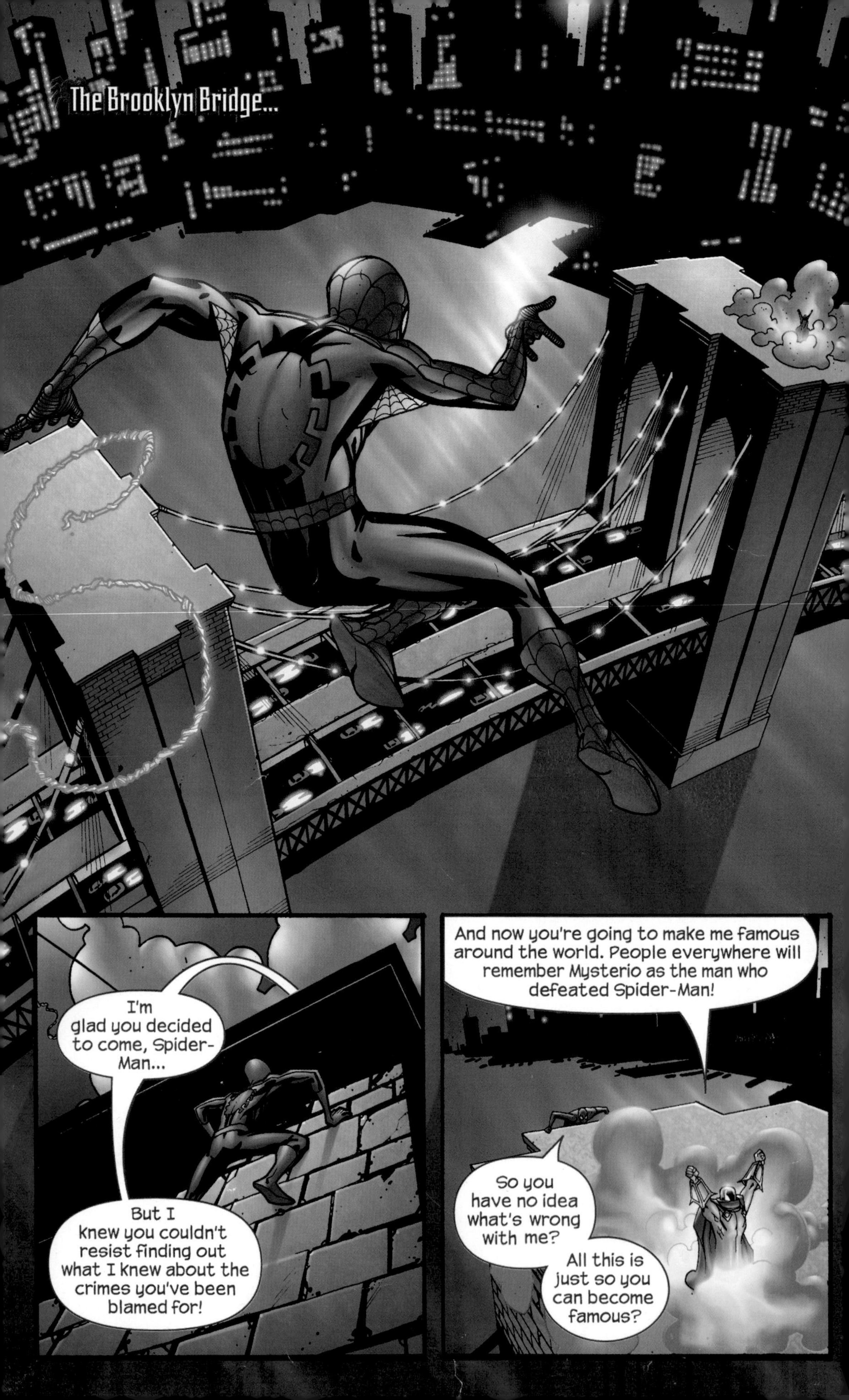
The Brooklyn Bridge...
I'm glad you decided to come, Spider-Man...
But I knew you couldn't resist finding out what I knew about the crimes you've been blamed for!
And now you're going to make me famous around the world. People everywhere will remember Mysterio as the man who defeated Spider-Man!
So you have no idea what's wrong with me?
All this is just so you can become famous?

Yes, I'll be famous and rich... but I never said I didn't know what's been wrong with you.
I do know the mystery behind your robberies...
...but for now we have to put on a show for the news 'copters.
Make sure you smile for the cameras.
Yeah. Keep talking!
Eat some webs!
THWIP
I have prepared for this moment.
You are out of your league.

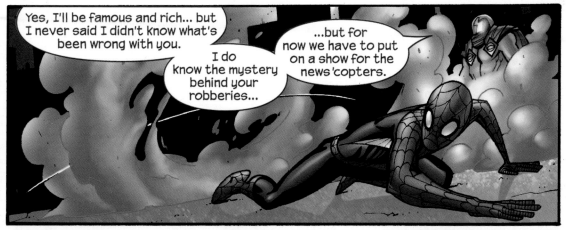

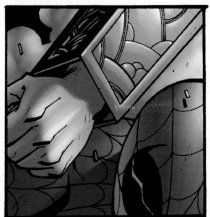

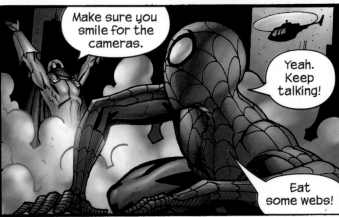

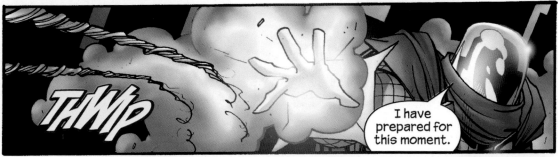

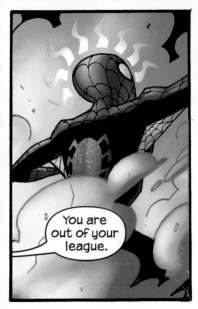

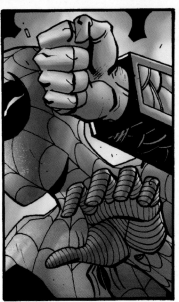

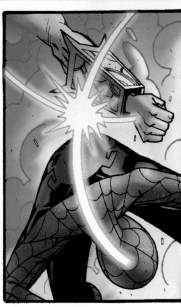

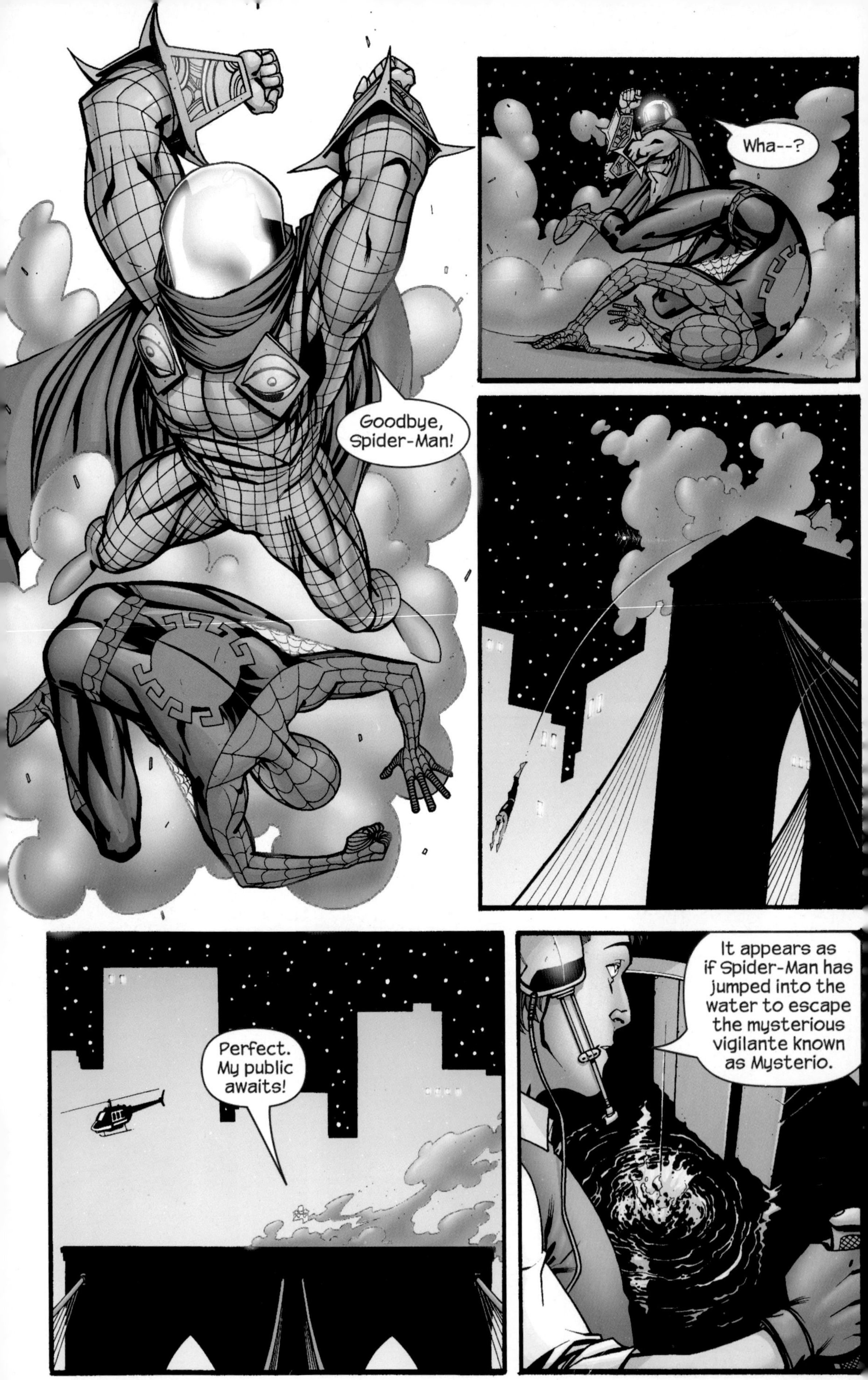
Goodbye, Spider-Man!
Wha--?
Perfect. My public awaits!
It appears as if Spider-Man has jumped into the water to escape the mysterious vigilante known as Mysterio.

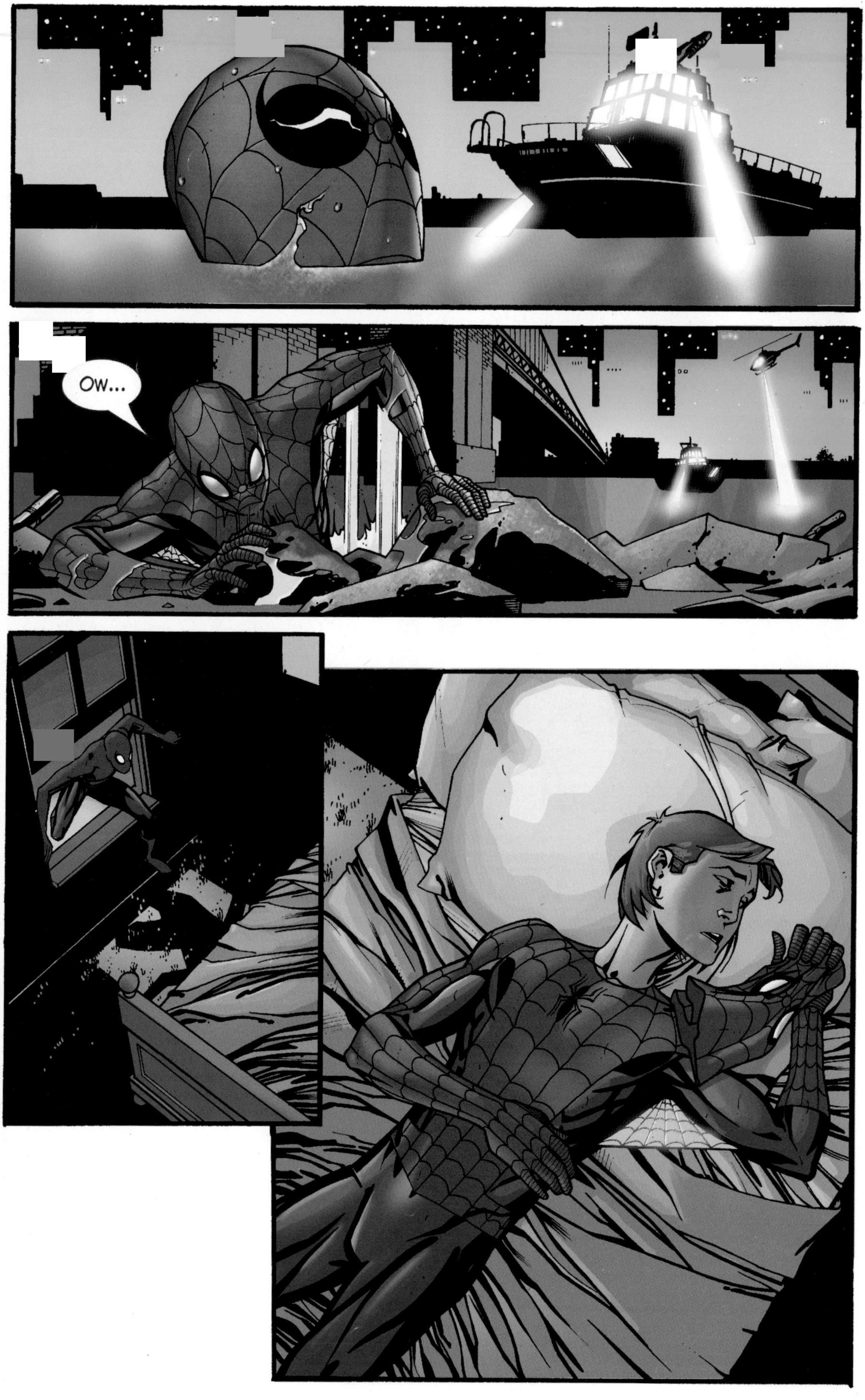
Ow...

OW...

Oh, Peter. I was just about to wake you up. You're running late.

I didn't even hear you come in last night.

Sorry, Aunt May. I was studying with some friends at the library.

We've got a tough calculus test today.

I'm sure you'll do fine.

Aunt May, can you turn that up?

Oh my, you probably didn't know with all your studying.

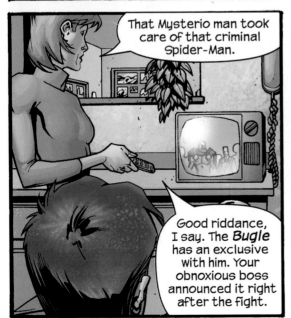

That Mysterio man took care of that criminal Spider-Man.

Good riddance, I say. The *Bugle* has an exclusive with him. Your obnoxious boss announced it right after the fight.

So, if you want to hear the real scoop about what happened between Spider-Man and Mysterio on that bridge you should pick up the *Daily Bugle* tomorrow morning.

This man is a hero.

BRING BRING

Hello?

Parker. Get down to the *Bugle*. I want you to take pictures today.

Oh, um I've got school--

Well, I thought I'd give you first crack since you needed some money.

I'll be right there.

Peter, you aren't going to miss school are you?

No, I'll go down there right now. I only have gym in the morning.

Not a class or anything. Can you write me a note?

Thanks, Aunt May. The money will help us out. It's an easy assignment!

Don't get too close to that Mysterio. They still haven't found Spider-Man's body in the river and he might go looking for revenge.

Could this get any worse?

Where've you been, Parker?

I came as fast as I could.

The Daily Bugle.

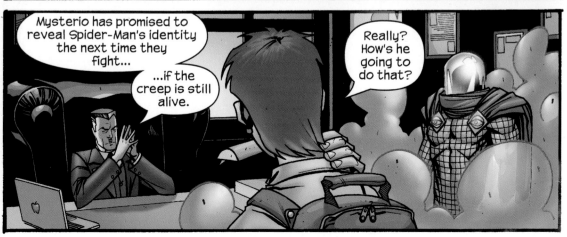

Mysterio has promised to reveal Spider-Man's identity the next time they fight...

...if the creep is still alive.

Really? How's he going to do that?

All will be revealed shortly.

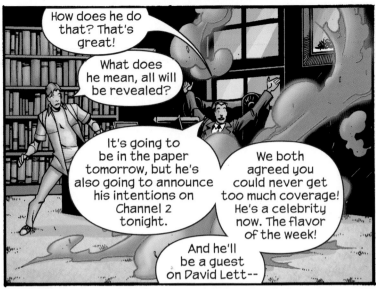

How does he do that? That's great!

What does he mean, all will be revealed?

It's going to be in the paper tomorrow, but he's also going to announce his intentions on Channel 2 tonight.

We both agreed you could never get too much coverage! He's a celebrity now. The flavor of the week!

And he'll be a guest on David Lett--

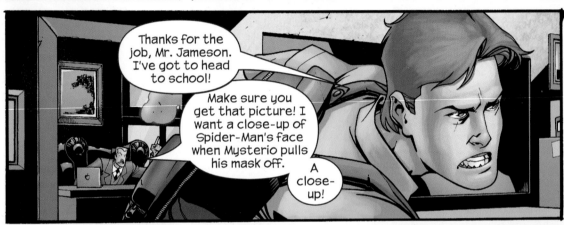

Thanks for the job, Mr. Jameson. I've got to head to school!

Make sure you get that picture! I want a close-up of Spider-Man's face when Mysterio pulls his mask off.

A close-up!

Later that night...

Oh, you've got to be kidding me. He's giving autographs?!?

Well, let's hope this works.

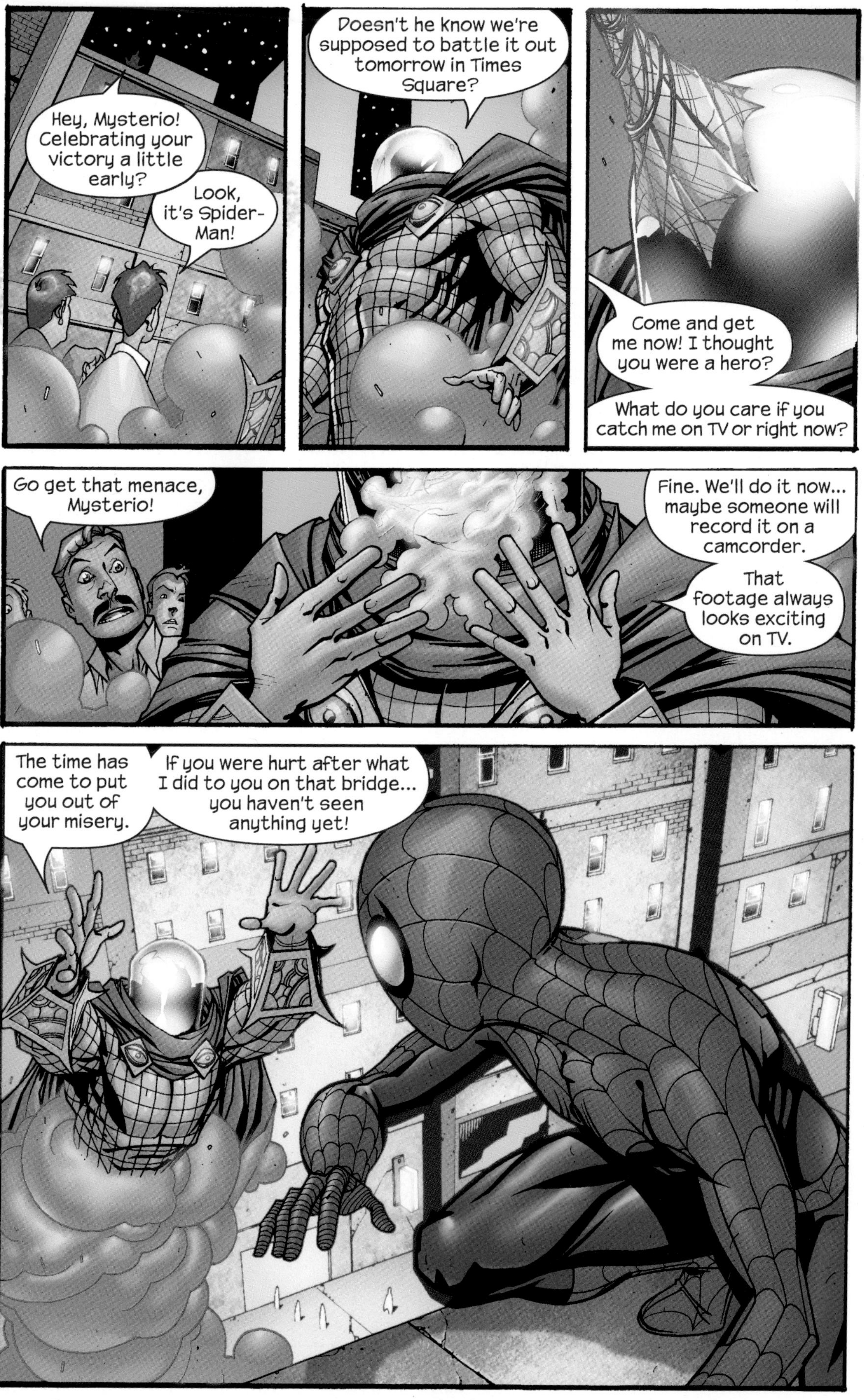
Hey, Mysterio! Celebrating your victory a little early?
Look, it's Spider-Man!
Doesn't he know we're supposed to battle it out tomorrow in Times Square?
Come and get me now! I thought you were a hero?
What do you care if you catch me on TV or right now?
Go get that menace, Mysterio!
Fine. We'll do it now... maybe someone will record it on a camcorder.
That footage always looks exciting on TV.
The time has come to put you out of your misery.
If you were hurt after what I did to you on that bridge... you haven't seen anything yet!

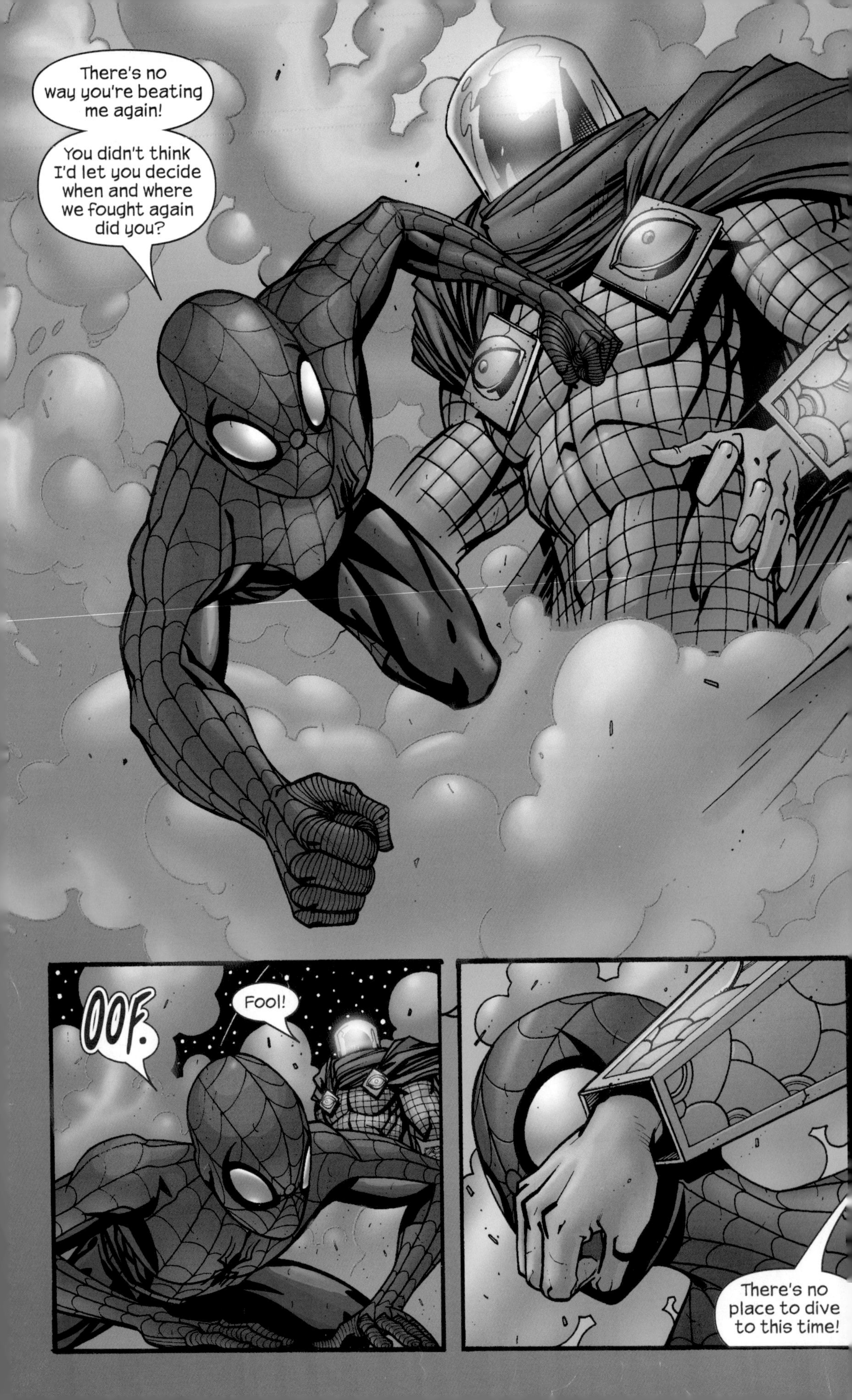
There's no way you're beating me again!
You didn't think I'd let you decide when and where we fought again did you?
OOF.
Fool!
There's no place to dive to this time!

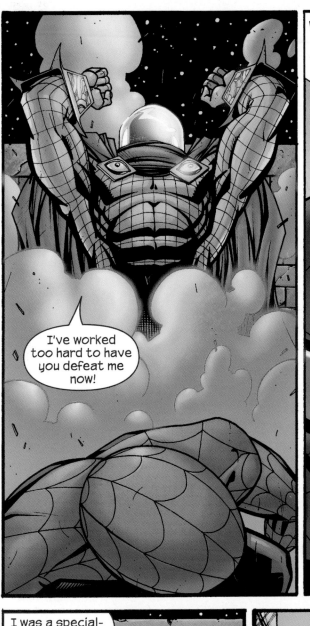

I've worked too hard to have you defeat me now!

Worked too hard at what? What does all of this have to do with my robbery spree?

You actually believed you were behind those robberies?

What did you think, you were Dr. Jekyll and Mr. Hyde when you went to bed?

I was a special-effects maker in Hollywood...

...I watched you on TV and wondered if I could do those things. Create props to help me perform those amazing stunts.

And I could.

So, you robbed all those places as me? But why become Mysterio?

Because after I used you to make the money I decided I wanted to be the hero, too.

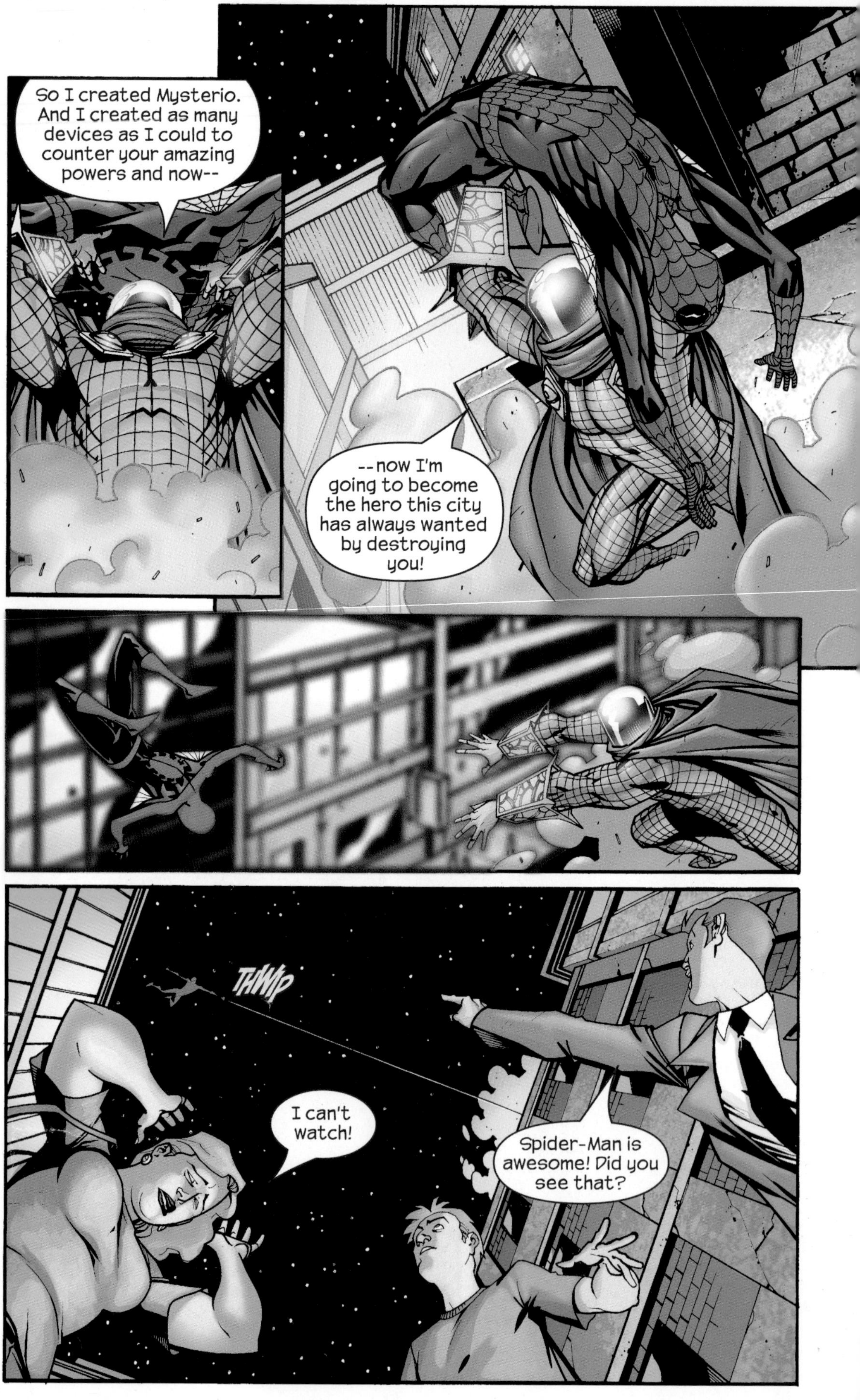
So I created Mysterio. And I created as many devices as I could to counter your amazing powers and now--
--now I'm going to become the hero this city has always wanted by destroying you!
THWIP
I can't watch!
Spider-Man is awesome! Did you see that?

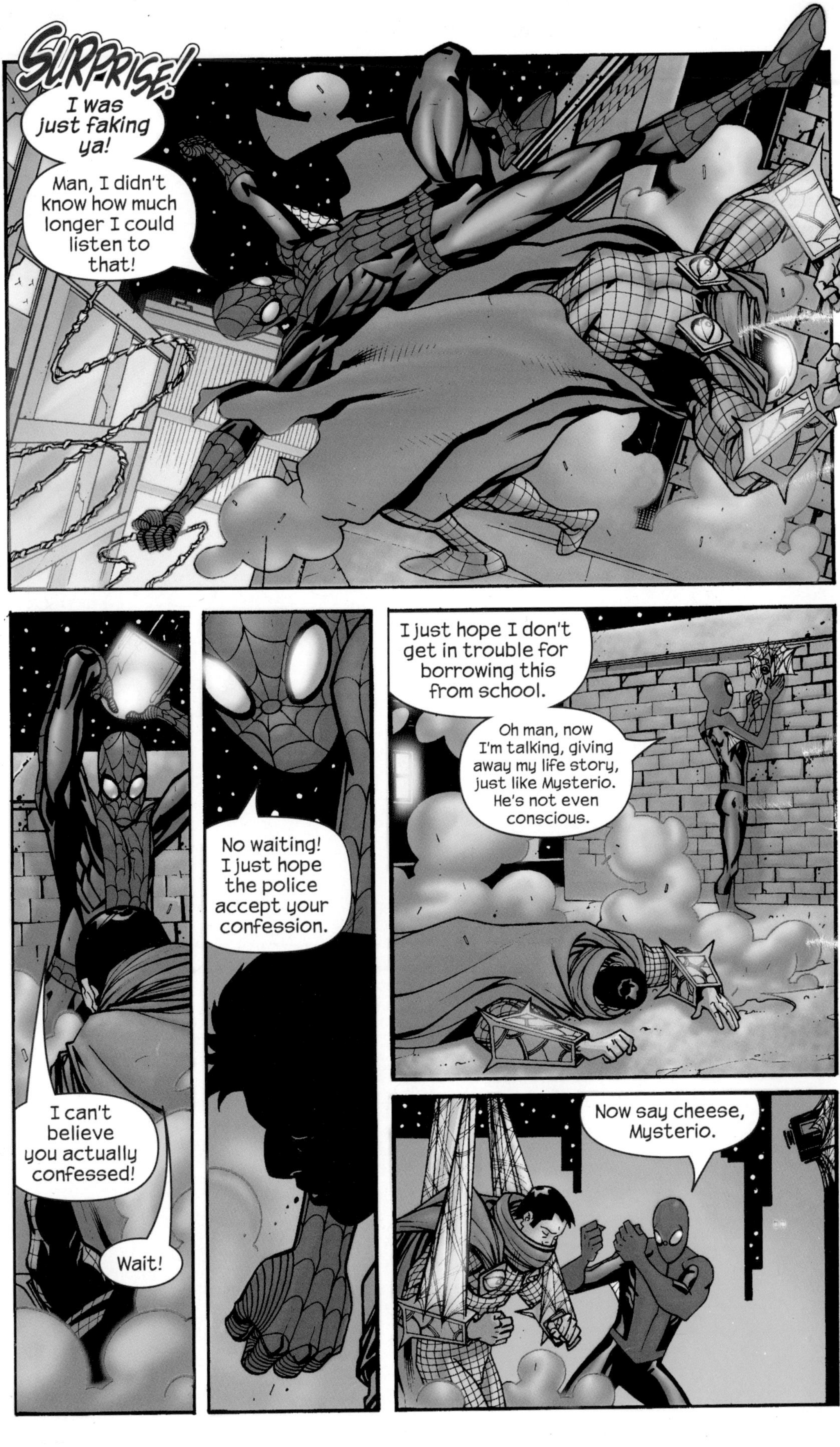
SURPRISE!
I was just faking ya!
Man, I didn't know how much longer I could listen to that!
I can't believe you actually confessed!
Wait!
No waiting! I just hope the police accept your confession.
I just hope I don't get in trouble for borrowing this from school.
Oh man, now I'm talking, giving away my life story, just like Mysterio. He's not even conscious.
Now say cheese, Mysterio.

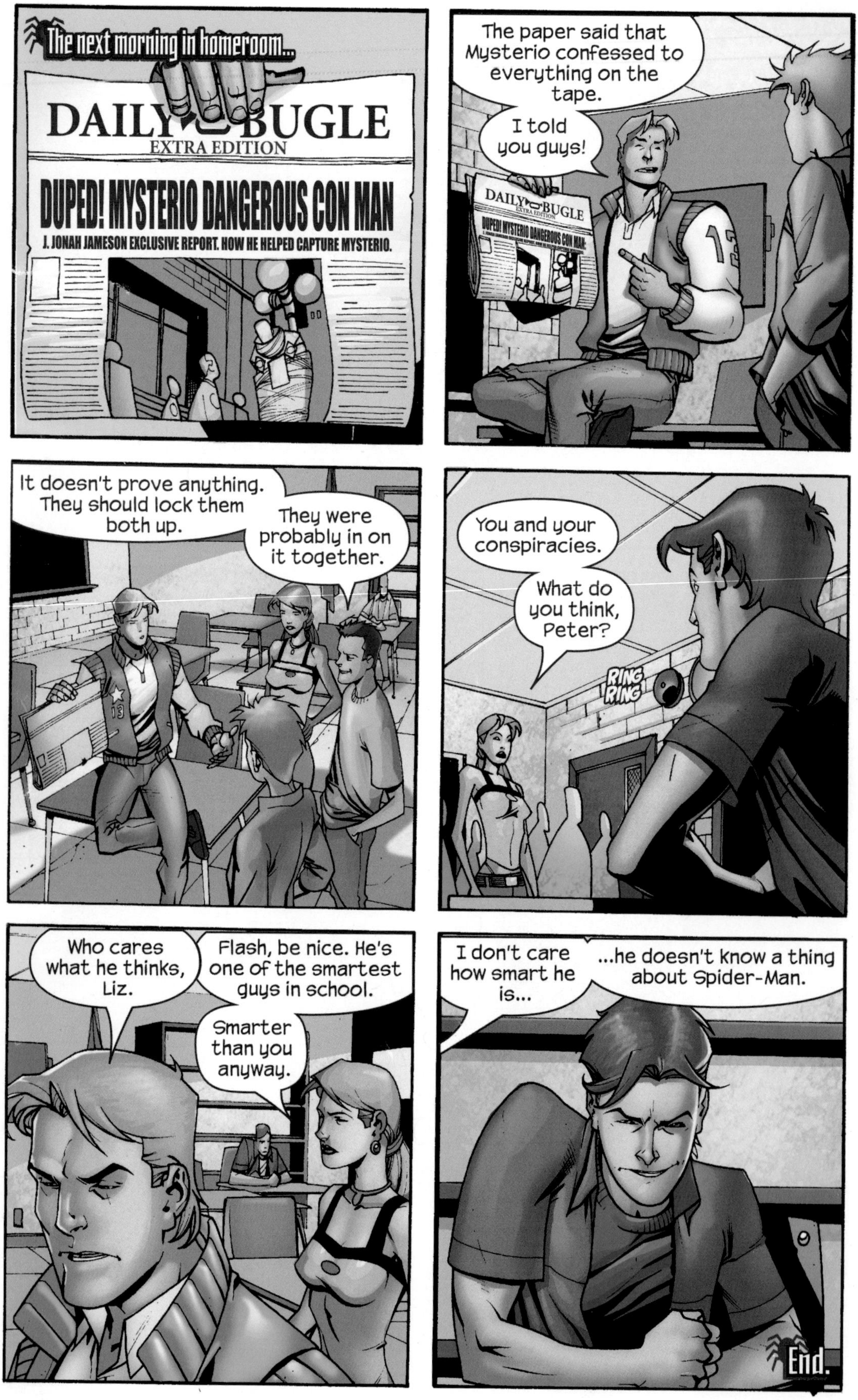
The next morning in homeroom...
DAILY BUGLE
EXTRA EDITION
DUPED! MYSTERIO DANGEROUS CON MAN
J. JONAH JAMESON EXCLUSIVE REPORT. HOW HE HELPED CAPTURE MYSTERIO.
The paper said that Mysterio confessed to everything on the tape.
I told you guys!
It doesn't prove anything. They should lock them both up.
They were probably in on it together.
You and your conspiracies.
What do you think, Peter?
RING RING
Who cares what he thinks, Liz.
Flash, be nice. He's one of the smartest guys in school.
Smarter than you anyway.
I don't care how smart he is...
...he doesn't know a thing about Spider-Man.
End.